MW00680600

ON THE
Merry-Go-Round

BY
bp NICHOL

PICTURES BY
SIMON NG

RED DEER COLLEGE PRESS

ACKNOWLEDGEMENTS
The publishers gratefully acknowledge the financial
assistance of the Alberta Foundation for the
Literary Arts, Alberta Culture & Multiculturalism,
and the Canada Council.

CREDITS
Designed by Michael Solomon, Toronto.
Typeset in Hiroshige by Merton Circle, Toronto.
Printed and bound in Singapore by Kyodo Printing
Company Pte. Ltd. for Red Deer College Press.

Canadian Cataloguing in Publication Data

Nichol, B. P., 1944-1988.
    On the merry-go-round

ISBN 0-88995-076-8

I. Ng, Simon. II. Title.
PS8527.I3205 1991   jC813'-54   C91-091242-4
PZ7.N520n 1991

On the Merry-Go-Round
the horse makes no sound,

but she takes me so far
and she takes me so high

I can ride to the edge of the sky.

On the Merry-Go-Round
the dog makes no sound,

but he runs on so swift
as I cling on his back

I can ride to the moon and ride back.

On the Merry-Go-Round
the deer makes no sound,

but she runs on so long
and she runs on so light

I can ride to the edge of the night.

On the Merry-Go-Round
if I make no sound

I'm the dog in his race

and the deer in her leap

and the horse that I'll ride into sleep,

and the horse that I'll ride into sleep.

ON THE MERRY-GO-ROUND

On the Merry-Go-Round
the horse makes no sound,
but she takes me so far
and she takes me so high
I can ride to the edge of the sky.

On the Merry-Go-Round
the dog makes no sound,
but he runs on so swift
as I cling on his back
I can ride to the moon and ride back.

On the Merry-Go-Round
the deer makes no sound,
but she runs on so long
and she runs on so light
I can ride to the edge of the night.

On the Merry-Go-Round
if I make no sound
I'm the dog in his race
and the deer in her leap
and the horse that I'll ride into sleep,
and the horse that I'll ride into sleep.